The
BIG BUCK
Adventure

$helley Gill and
Deborah Tobola

Illu$trated by
Grace Lin

TALEWIND$

A Charle$bridge Imprint

Published by Charlesbridge Publishing
85 Main Street, Watertown, MA 02472
(617) 926-0329
www.charlesbridge.com

Library of Congress Cataloging-in-Publication Data
Gill, Shelley.
The big buck adventure/Shelley Gill and Deborah Tobola; illustrated by Grace Lin.
p.   cm.
Summary: Rhyming account of a little girl's quandary as she tries to decide what
she can get with her dollar in a candy shop, toy store, deli, and pet department.
ISBN 0-88106-294-4 (reinforced for library use)
1. Mathematics Juvenile literature. 2. Money Juvenile literature.
[1. Mathematics. 2. Money.] I. Tobola, Deborah. II. Lin, Grace, ill. III. Title.
QA40.5.G55   2000
513—dc21   99-13393

Printed in the United States of America
(hc) 10 9 8 7 6 5 4 3 2 1

The illustrations in this book were done in gouache on Canson watercolor paper.
The display type and text type were set in Stone Sans and Myriad Tilt.
Color separations were made by Eastern Rainbow, Derry, New Hampshire.
Printed and bound by Worzalla Publishing Company, Stevens Point, Wisconsin
Production supervision by Brian G. Walker
Designed by Diane M. Earley
This book was printed on recycled paper.

To my pop, John Gill, who always knew the value of a buck
—S. G.

To Courtney Heard and her little purple purse
—D. T.

For my dad, who no longer has any big bucks because he spent them all on me
—G. L.

Saturday morning, I sure am in luck!
A raise in allowance—I get a buck!

Dad drops me at the store
with a new green bill.
He says, "I'll be back at a quarter 'til."

I rush to the candy counter,
my head held high.
I flash my moola.
"Please, what can this buy?"

Mr. Cash squints his eyes,
then straightens his collar.

Why, you could buy a hundred jawbreakers for a dollar!

"Tutti-frutti tongue twisters
cost one penny each
in tangerine, lemon-lime,
melon, and peach."

But I see gummy bears
crammed in a jar,
and I ask Mr. Cash
how much those are.

"Three for a quarter, kid,
one for a dime.
You can figure it out.
Just take your time."

Four quarters times three equals
twelve gummy bear treats,
a much better deal
than ten at ten cents each.

Over in toys I spy skates,
trains, and tracks,
rings and stilts and
sets of jacks.

I've got my eye on
a funny stuffed bunny,
but Miss Silver says,

Sorry, not enough money.

$5.

How about a half-dozen creepy night crawlers? on sale right now—six for a dollar!

I dart into the deli
with a fistful of dough
to see where else
my money can go.

$5.00

"Howdy, Ms. Penny. What can I buy?"
"Ooh! How 'bout a slice of hot apple pie?

One shiny nickel,
a giant dill pickle!

One quarter, beef jerky.

Three quarters,
leg o' turkey."

In the pet department
there's a plant that eats flies,
and a fuzzy white rat with
black feet and pink eyes.

Mr. Buck has three guppies
for one dollar bill.
He wants eighty-five cents
for ants and a hill.

"Don't want to spend that much?
How about a pet flea
or fly
or such?

They're three for a penny,
not a cent more—
Best doggone deal
in the whole darn store!"

I figure the math:
thirty-three cents for each fish.
One hundred times three—
more fleas than I wish!

I leave Mr. Buck with
his fleas and his flies
and go stand in housewares
and close my eyes.

Now I wish I didn't have
so much money.
At first this was fun,
now it's not even funny!

What to choose?
One hundred tongue twisters,
tangerine and peach?
Or ten sticky gummy bears
at ten cents each?

Six worms or some jerky?
Three guppies or turkey?

Ants for three quarters
and two nickels?
Or all my cash
for twenty giant pickles?

I've had it.

I can't stand it.

I can't take any more!

I know I'm supposed
to behave in a store,

But I stride to the middle
of the place, and I holler,
"What in the world should
I buy with my dollar?"

They come running:
Cash, Silver, Buck, and Penny.
Clutching my bill I yell,

I don't want

My head is spinning with what
I could have bought

When Miss Silver asks,

penny for your thoughts?

Slowly I turn and say like a scholar,
"Why you can have one hundred
of my thoughts for a dollar!

Ten thoughts for a dime,
five for a nickel,
twenty-five thoughts
for a sour dill pickle.

Three for a quarter
is not the best deal,

but flea-thoughts
and fly-thoughts

are really a steal!"

My father walks in.

Hi, honey! Any luck?

I just have to laugh
as I pocket my buck.